Lee Aucoin, *Creative Director*
Jamey Acosta, *Senior Editor*
Heidi Fiedler, *Editor*
Produced and designed by
Denise Ryan & Associates
Illustration © Susy Boyer
Rachelle Cracchiolo, *Publisher*

Teacher Created Materials

5301 Oceanus Drive
Huntington Beach, CA 92649-1030
http://www.tcmpub.com
Paperback: ISBN: 978-1-4333-5454-0
Library Binding: ISBN: 978-1-4807-1133-4

Boris
the Basset

Written by Sharon Callen
Illustrated by Susy Boyer

Boris is a grumpy dog.

3

He does not like wild, windy days.

He does not like bright, sunny days.

He does not like cold, snowy days.

He does not like hot, humid days.

10

What kind of days does Boris like?
He really likes indoor days!